Cardiff Libraries
www.cardiff.gov.uk/libraries

Llyfrgelloedd Cae
www.cae.dydd.gov.uk/llyfr

D0231611

BOTHERSOME BRAMBLES

HOME

GUSTY HILL

PUNTING RIVER

DANK CAVE

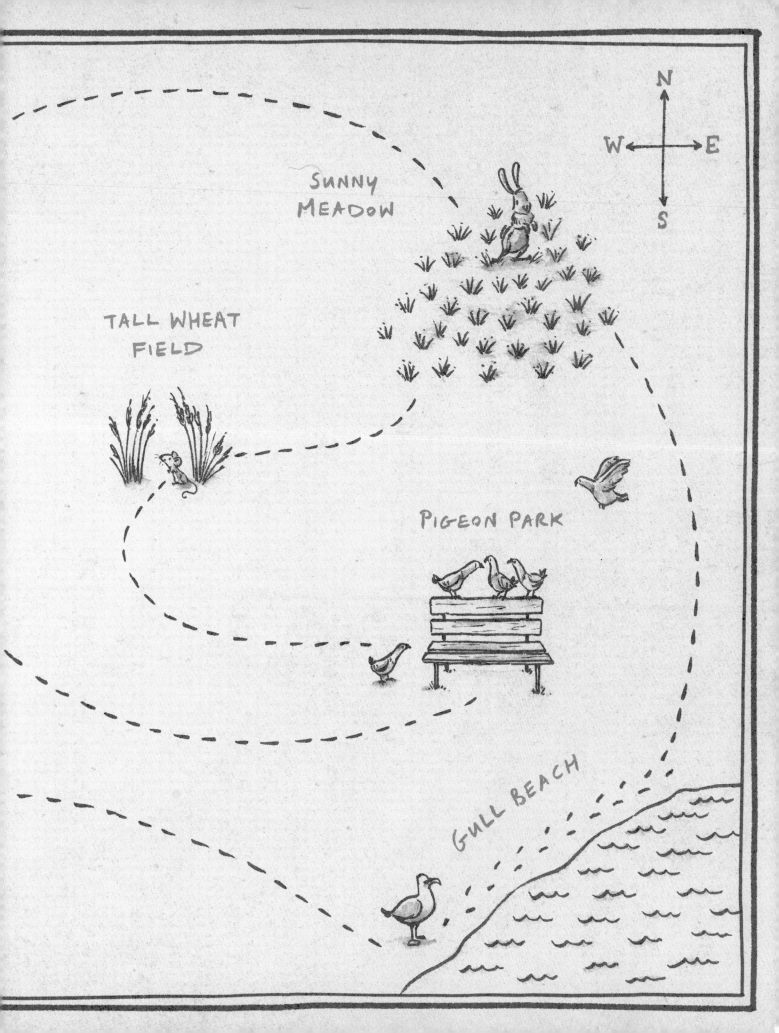

SUNNY
MEADOW

TALL WHEAT
FIELD

PIGEON PARK

GULL BEACH

N
W E
S

For Mum and Dad xx

A TEMPLAR BOOK

First published in the UK in 2016 by Templar Publishing,

part of the Bonnier Publishing Group,

The Plaza, 535 King's Road, London, SW10 0SZ

www.templarco.co.uk

www.bonnierpublishing.com

Copyright © 2016 by Ciara Flood

1 3 5 7 9 10 8 6 4 2

All rights reserved

ISBN 978-1-78370-238-1 Hardback

ISBN 978-1-78370-239-8 Paperback

Edited by Katie Haworth

Printed in China

the
PERFECT
PICNIC

Ciara Flood

templar publishing

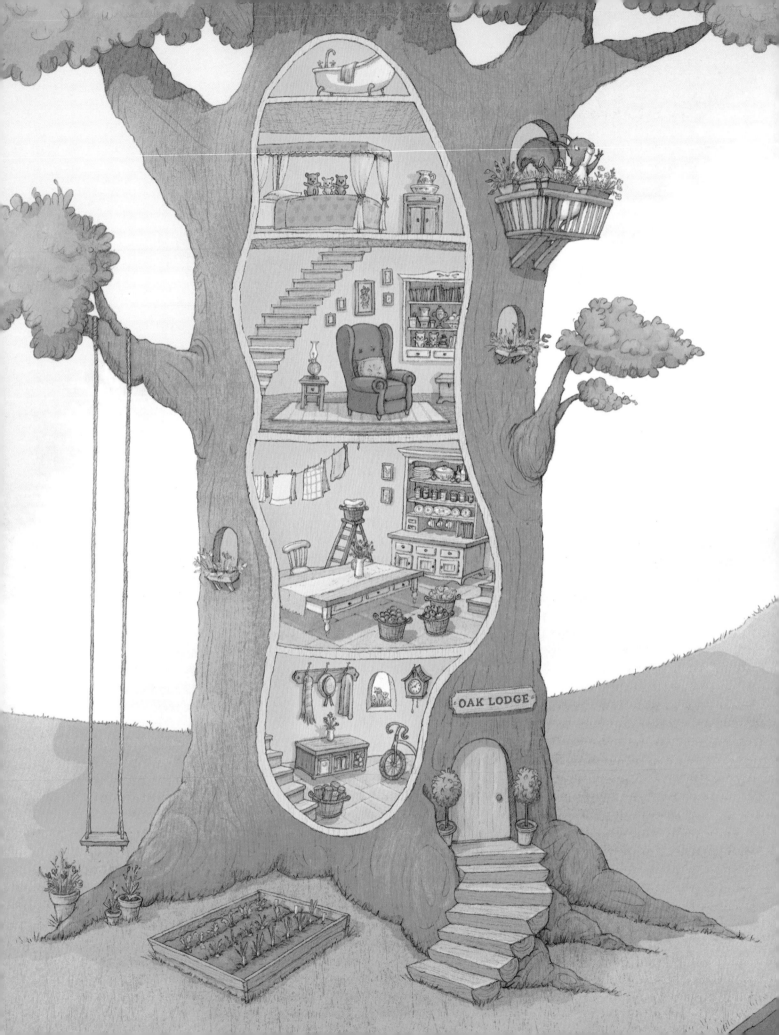

OAK LODGE

Squirrel and Mole were the best of friends.

They did everything together.
They danced together,

they baked cakes together,

they went on bike rides together

and they especially liked
to paint pictures together.

One day Squirrel and Mole decided to go on
a picnic. Squirrel wanted it to be the most
perfect picnic ever.

"No butter on the sandwiches!" said Squirrel.
"Right you are, Squirrel," said Mole
(even though he loved butter
on his sandwiches).

After much fussing everything
was ready to go into the picnic bag ...

… and off they went.

"Don't worry, Mole," said Squirrel.

"I'm going to find us the
perfect place for our picnic."

"Right you are," said Mole.

RrrrriiiPPPP!

"This is a very pretty meadow," said Mole.
"Yes, but it's not perfect," said Squirrel.
"We need more shade."
"Right you are," said Mole.

"This has shade," said Mole.
"Yes, but there's too
much of it," said Squirrel.
"Right you are," said Mole.

"Well, how about here?" asked Mole.

"It's far too busy," said Squirrel.
"Right you are," said Mole.

"There's nobody else up here," said Mole.
"Yes, but it's much too windy," said Squirrel.
"Right you are," sighed Mole.

The two friends went
to a lot of places ...

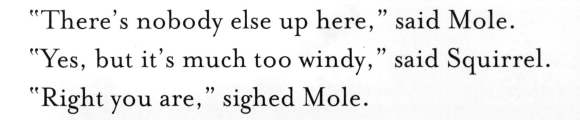

... a river,

"Too wet ..."

a cave,

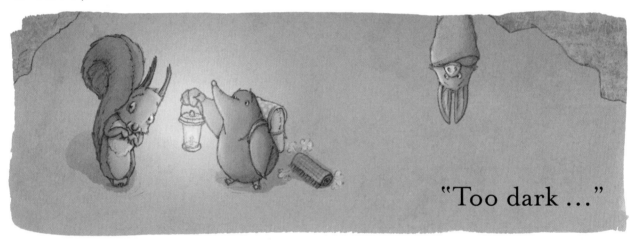

"Too dark ..."

a beach,

"Too sandy ..."

... until Squirrel finally stopped.

"I've found it, Mole!" she said.
"The perfect place to have our picnic."

"But Squirrel, we've already been here!"
groaned Mole.

Mole then noticed something else.
"Uh-oh!" he said.

OOOOO!"

wailed Squirrel.
"This is the worst picnic ever!"

"Ahem!" said a small voice.

"I believe this is your cake?" said Mouse.

"And these are your apples," said Otter.

"I found your rug," said Bat.

"I have your sandwiches," said Seagull.

"And we have your cracker," said the Pigeons.

"Here are your plates," said Goat.

"And is anyone looking for a nice cup of tea?" asked Hare.

The apples were bruised, the cake
was squashed, the plates were chipped,
the forks and spoons were bent, the rug was dusty,
the sandwiches were sandy, the tea was cold
and the crackers were very much eaten.

"Don't worry, Squirrel," said Mole.
"We can fix this."

It was not the perfect picnic that
Squirrel had planned,

but it was a lot of fun!

"I'm already looking forward to our next picnic,"
said Squirrel.

"Me too," said Mole. "But next time,
let's have butter on the sandwiches."

"Right you are, Mole," said Squirrel.
"Right you are."

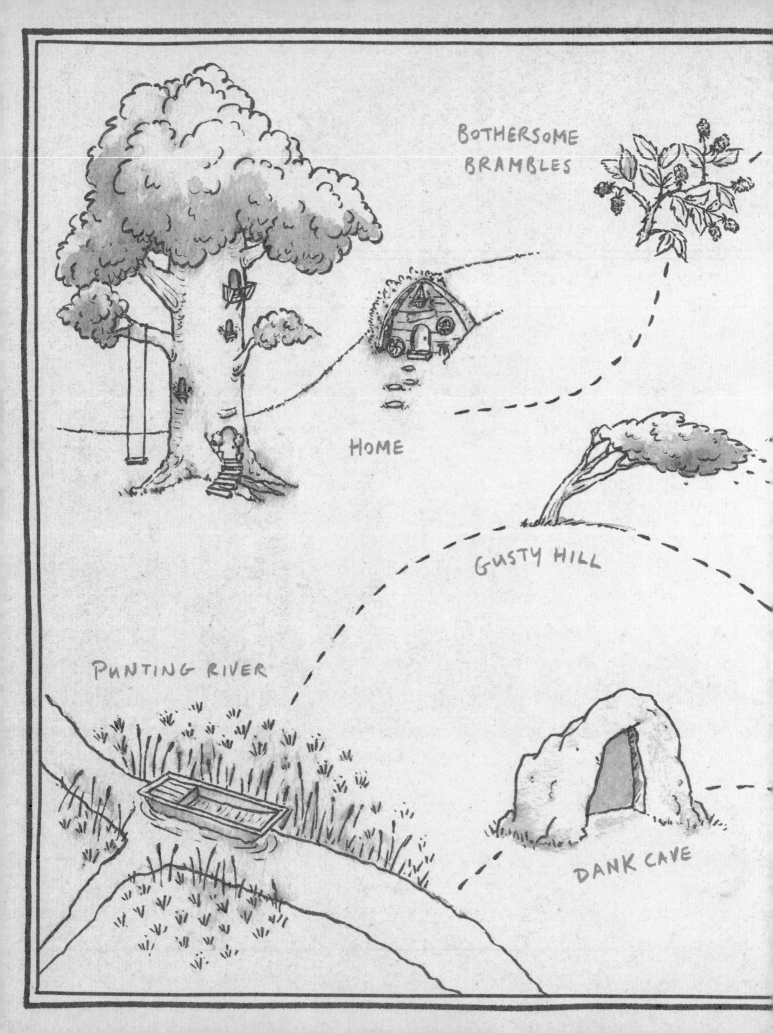

BOTHERSOME
BRAMBLES

HOME

GUSTY HILL

PUNTING RIVER

DANK CAVE

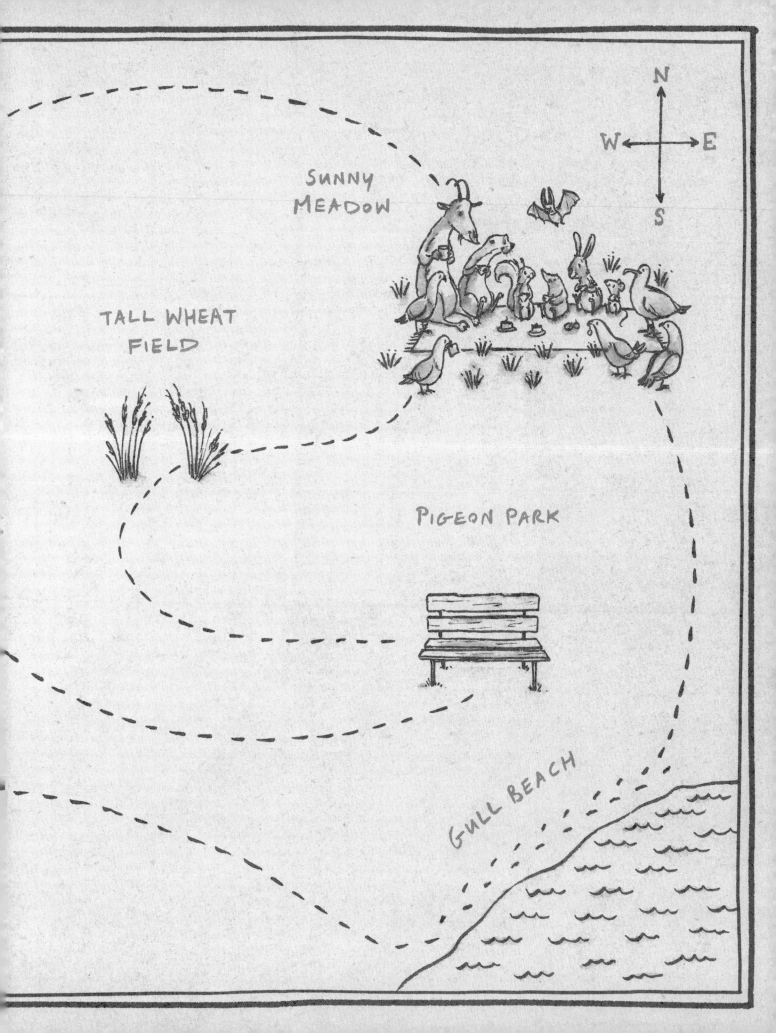

SUNNY
MEADOW

TALL WHEAT
FIELD

PIGEON PARK

GULL BEACH

N
W
E
S